Good Night, Good Knight

BY **Shelley Moore Thomas**

PiCTURES BY **Jennifer Plecas**

SCHOLASTIC INC.

New York Toronto London Auckland Sydney
Mexico City New Delhi Hong Kong Buenos Aires

ISBN 0-439-39010-9

Text copyright © 2000 by Shelley Moore Thomas.
Illustrations copyright © 2000 by Jennifer Plecas.
All rights reserved.
Published by Scholastic Inc., 555 Broadway, New York, NY 10012,
by arrangement with Dutton Children's Books, a division of Penguin Putnam Inc.
SCHOLASTIC and associated logos are trademarks
and/or registered trademarks of Scholastic Inc.

12 11 10 9 8 7 6 5 4 3   2 3 4 5 6 7/0

Printed in the U.S.A.   23

First Scholastic printing, January 2002

For Nana and Papa John,
who know all about dragons
S.M.T.

For S.U.
J.P.

Once there were three little dragons.

They lived in a dark cave.

The cave was in a dense forest.

The forest was in a faraway kingdom.

The poor little dragons

were very lonely

in their deep dark cave.

5

In the kingdom

there was a Good Knight.

Every night he kept watch.

He watched from

a crumbly tumbly tower.

It was on top

of a very tall wall.

One night the Good Knight

was on his watch.

He heard a very large,

very loud roar.

So the Good Knight

left the crumbly tumbly tower.

He climbed down the very tall wall.

He jumped on his horse.

"Away!" he said.

He galloped through the king's forest.

Clippety-clop. Clippety-clop.

He came to the deep dark cave.

Inside he saw the first little dragon.

"What's this?" he asked.

"Methinks it is a dragon!"

And he drew his

shimmery, glimmery sword.

The dragon had on his jammies.

He was all ready for bed.

"Oh good. You have come,"

said the dragon.

"Could you bring me

a drink of water?

Please.

Then I can go to sleep."

The Good Knight did not know

what to think.

But he was a good knight.

So he got a drink of water.

He gave it to the dragon.

Then he tucked him into bed.

"Good night, good dragon.

Sleep well, sleep tight,"

said the Good Knight.

Then he galloped away.

The Good Knight went back

through the king's forest.

Clippety-clop.

Clippety-clop.

He got off his horse.

Thud.

He climbed up the very tall wall

to the crumbly tumbly tower.

There he stood on watch.

He stood on watch

for five minutes.

Then he heard another

very large,

very loud roar.

15

"I don't believe this,"

he said.

He left the crumbly tumbly tower.

He climbed down the very tall wall.

He jumped on his horse.

"Away!" he cried.

He galloped through the king's forest.

Clippety-clop. Clippety-clop.

He came to the deep dark cave.

The second dragon was in her jammies.

She was all ready for bed.

"Oh good. You have come,"

said the second dragon.

"Could you read me a story?

Please.

Then I can go to sleep."

"And could I have

another drink of water?"

said the first dragon.

The Good Knight did not know

what to think.

But he was a good knight.

So he read the dragon a story.

Then he tucked her into bed.

He got the first dragon

another drink of water.

Then he tucked him into bed.

"Good night, good dragons.

Sleep well, sleep tight,"

said the Good Knight.

Then he galloped away.

The Good Knight went back

through the king's forest.

Clippety-clop.

Clippety-clop.

He got off his horse.

Thud.

He climbed up the very tall wall

to the crumbly tumbly tower.

There he stood on watch.

He stood on watch

for two minutes.

Then he heard another

very large,

very loud roar.

"This is too much,"

he said.

He left the crumbly tumbly tower.

He climbed down the very tall wall.

He jumped on his horse.

"Away!" he cried.

He galloped through the king's forest.

Clippety-clop. Clippety-clop.

He came to the deep dark cave.

The third dragon had

on his jammies.

He was all ready for bed.

"Oh good. You have come,"

said the third dragon.

"Could you sing me a song?

Please.

Then I can go to sleep."

"And could you read me

another story?"

said the second dragon.

"And could you get me

another drink of water?"

said the first dragon.

The Good Knight did not know

what to think.

But he was a good knight.

So he sang the dragon a song.

Then he tucked him into bed.

He read the second dragon

another story.

Then he tucked her into bed.

He got the first dragon

another drink of water.

Then he tucked him into bed.

"Good night, good dragons.

Sleep well, sleep tight,"

said the Good Knight.

Then he galloped away.

The Good Knight went back

through the king's forest.

Clippety-clop.

Clippety-clop.

He got off his horse.

Thud.

He climbed up the very tall wall

to the crumbly tumbly tower.

There he stood watch.

He stood on watch

for one minute.

Then he heard

the largest, loudest roar of all.

"Not again,"

he said.

He left the crumbly tumbly tower.

He climbed down the very tall wall.

He jumped on his horse.

"Away!" he cried.

He galloped through the king's forest.

Clippety-clop. Clippety-clop.

He came to the deep dark cave.

"Oh good. You have come,"

said all three dragons.

"Let me guess,"

said the Good Knight.

"Another drink of water?"

"No," said the first dragon.

"Another story?"

"No," said the second dragon.

"Another song?"

"No," said the third dragon.

"Then WHAT DO YOU WANT?"

cried the Good Knight.

"We need a good-night kiss,"

said the little dragons.

And they lifted

their scaly little cheeks.

"This is going too far,"

said the Good Knight.

But he was a good knight.

So he bent and kissed

each scaly little cheek.

"Good night, good dragons.

Sleep well, sleep tight,"

he said.

The dragons said,

"Good night, Good Knight."

The Good Knight left the cave.

He waited outside.

He heard the loud dragon snores.

Then the Good Knight went home

through the king's forest.

Clippety-clop. Clippety-clop.

He got off his horse.

Thud.

"Now," said the Good Knight,

"maybe I can get a

good night's sleep."

And that is just

what he did.

Sleep well, sleep tight,

Good Knight.